I0772739

THE GPS

K. D. Blackstone

CONTENTS

CHAPTER 1

Dylan has never been to that part of the neighborhood, but he would willingly do anything to please Kayla. They've been dating for two weeks and could not keep their hands off each other. He would have explored his opportunity, but Kayla's parents were strict and would never support her dating while in college.

"Why does your father hate me?" Dylan randomly asked Kayla.

She leaned forward and kissed him on his lips. "Because they just don't understand what a spectacular man you are."

Dylan knew the truth, and it wasn't related to what Kayla said. Her parents didn't like him because he was a delivery boy and didn't have wealthy parents like the kind of man they wished she dated. He remembered days when Kayla would cancel out on him because she was attending a socialite party with other guys.

"You have to make a choice," Dylan said to Kayla, when they later saw each other.

"Let's not do this," Kayla sighed, shaking her head. She was never one to make tough choices, and she always wanted others to be pleased with her. She believed there were other ways to go about things without hurting anyone emotionally.

They set a time to sneak away and meet, but it had to be away from home. This particular night they met in Dylan's old car, an 'i miss you" had them kissing and running hands all over their bodies.

"Let's get out of here," Dylan told Kayla, and she nodded.

He drove them to a distant neighborhood, closer to the woods, where they could enjoy all forms of exploration without interruptions. As soon as Dylan hit the brakes, Kayla sat in his lap, facing him and blocking his view. She pulled up his shirt, peppering him with kisses over his body. Dylan also pulled off her shirt, leaving her in a black bra and jeans. It was a pleasurable and enjoyable moment until they heard a sound and looked up to see a car driving towards them with full headlights. Dylan pushed Kayla off him, waited until the car got to where they were, and stopped. It was a police officer.

"Hello, kids," he greeted. He was a bespectacled older man. "What are you doing here at this hour of the day?" He glanced at his watch. "What's your name?" he asked Kayla.

"Kay-"she replied.

"Why you gon' give him info about yourself?" Dylan muttered. He didn't like police officers one bit. He knew that the officer was trouble. He could sense it.

"Kay what, the officer asked?"

"Kayla". she answered reluctantly.

"I'll be back on patrol in ten minutes, and if I find you here; you're going to the station with me, is that clear?" The officer said in a firm voice.

Dylan said something under his breath, and Kayla frowned at him.

"What did you say, kid?" The officer snapped.

"Nothing, man," Dylan replied.

"Good, now, pray I don't find you here when I return." Then, he drove off, leaving them by the roadside leading into the woods.

"What was that?" Dylan asked, pushing Kayla's hand off his leg.

"What was what?" She sounded confused.

"Why didn't you give him your personal information? Huh, you could have given him that also."

"Dylan..."

Dylan was more annoyed because the man told them to go home, and he knew Kayla was not anti-establishment like him. He hated the police and all the government bureaucracy. He would have stayed right there and dared the officer to come back but he knew she was likely to suggest they go back home.

He kept quiet, staring ahead of him. He waited for Kayla to say something before he could know his next move.

"Do you want to go home?" She asked, while rubbing his leg and kissing him on his neck.

He smiled. "Do you want to?"

"Uhm uhm, I want to spend more time with you, but we could get caught," she separated from him, staring at him in the dark.

He could see her facial expression, but he knew she would agree with his suggestion if he gave one.

"Let's go somewhere else," he said.

Kayla moved away from Dylan and sat in the passenger seat by his side. "Let's go."

Dylan roared the engine to life. He planned to drive into the woods, no one would see them there, and they could spend more time with each other. They drove off the road into the woods, following a straight path. It was dark, and there was no one or any light in sight.

"Where are we?" Kayla asked in a quiet tone.

"The GPS will help us out," Dylan said confidently. He ignored the creeps he got from being in the woods in the dark. They had nothing to fear.

He turned the GPS on and the voice started, "Follow the route". Then, suddenly, Kayla gripped him tight by his arm.

"Did you see that?" She asked, her voice laced with fear and panic.

"What is that?" He peered into the dark from the windshield, but he couldn't see anything.

"Something just moved past us. A shape, it was almost unreal", Kayla said. "Dylan, I think this is a bad idea. Let's go home," she said, tightening her seatbelt.

"It's nothing. Your imaginations are messing with you," he chuckled when he saw something like a shadow run past the car.

"Dylan?" Kayla was almost crying.

Dylan started the car, following the GPS when it directed them towards the left. It seemed to be the only help they had at the moment. So they followed it for some minutes until Kayla realized something.

"Hey Dylan, are we following the GPS?"

"Yes," he answered, concentrating on the dark narrow path in front of them. "The GPS is correct."

"Why are we back to where we started from?" Kayla didn't understand, and she needed a valid explanation.

"Wait, I must have been the one making a mistake. The GPS says left," they glance at the two paths, "Left, let's go left." Dylan turned left and the GPS loudly glared, "Recalculating. . . . Recalculating. . .`` "Maybe we should go right," Dylan said, confused.

"Do you have any idea where we are headed at all?" Kayla asked.

Dylan kept driving with his eyes fixed on the GPS. He believed in no time they would be out of there. It wasn't until Kayla screamed that he realized they were far from being safe. They couldn't see anything but darkness in front of them. Kayla looked outside, adjusting her eyes, and spoke in a panic-stricken voice. "I think...we drove to a cliff."

"Shit!" Dylan was shocked. "He tried to reverse the car, but the GPS kept glaring loudly, "Recalculating. . . . Recalculating. . ." It seemed as if it had taken control of the car and moving them forward.

Kayla turned to Dylan, confused and shocked. The car wouldn't respond to Dylan. Instead, it moved in the GPS's direction, jerking them forward towards the cliff's edge. Kayla did the first thing she could think of, she pushed the door by her side, but it wouldn't budge. The GPS glared, "Recalculating. . . . Recalculating. . ". Dylan also tried to force the door open. He struggled with it until their car was almost tipping off.

"What the fuck is going on?!" Dylan screamed.

"I don't know. We are going to die!" Her eyes were glistening with tears as she pushed her seat backward.

She sniffed and kept hitting the door. The car rattled with their hearts in their throats. This wasn't the end they thought they would have, but the vehicle tipped off in the blink of an eye, and their screams filled the air. They wished it was a nightmare, and perhaps it would have been, if they were separated from their bodies, staring lifelessly at the world that was once theirs.

* * * * * *

FIVE MONTHS LATER

"Mom! Greg is being annoying," Jules cried. This was the third time she would report her twin to her mom, and nothing was done.

"Greg," their mom said in a quiet yet threatening voice, "I will not repeat myself. If you keep it up, you'll have to spend the next road trip with Aunt Jane."

"Mom," Greg grunted. That was the worst option any of the Brandice children could have. It was an unspoken rule, but no one could ever misbehave to an extent where they would have to spend time with Aunt Jane. She was the meanest lady anyone had ever met. She would spend hours complaining about everything. Anytime children stayed at her house, she would make them spend hours working as if they were her maid.

She didn't have a TV or any electronics that people have in modern homes. Only "boring books about psychology", as Greg recalled from his last punishment at her house.

"Apologize to your sister."

"Mom…"

"Honey, I think we should consider-"

"Jules, I'm sorry," Greg said quickly. He knew his mom could persuade their dad to do anything, and it would be wrong if he would have to go to Aunt Jane's. Jules gave Greg a face as if to say, 'that serves you right,' as he glared at her.

Sean Brandice had his sleepy eyes fixed on the road with the light and noises of Greg and Jules' phones behind him and Dawn Brandice, his wife, seated next to him.

"Are you sure we are on the right path?" Dawn asked, ignoring the noise that came from the kids. They had been on the road for hours, trying to locate a camping spot, but they've not been able to do that. It became more frustrating by the minute.

"Can I get more coffee, please?" Sean asked.

Dawn looked at him with surprise. "Would you like me to drive? You look tired."

"What's more tiring is more miles on this road and not finding our camp site yet. This is the first time we've ever been lost this badly," he said sheepishly to Dawn.

"Mom, when will we get there?" Greg asked, his voice filled with curiosity.

"Soon, darling. Soon…" She assured him.

There had been no other vehicle on the road except theirs, and that alone bothered them. However, Sean believed they would find their destination soon. They probably had taken the wrong path.

"Turn on the GPS. It would help us a bit. I don't know why you're being stubborn," Dawn complained.

The kids became quiet behind them. It wasn't funny anymore, seeing as they had gotten lost on the road.

Sean sighed and turned on the GPS. He rarely used it, but it would prove itself useful at least. Sean liked to read maps and chart his directions like he did in the Boy Scouts when he was a Scout Master. However, he did as Dawn said and waited for the GPS to pop-up their current location before he clicked on their destination. A red line spiraled across the edge of the screen to show how far they were from the campsite.

"That's a lot," Dawn blinked with wide eyes. She yawned because she was exhausted, and like her husband, she also needed to sleep. Unfortunately, none of them could do that yet. The road wasn't safe. Luckily, they now had the GPS to guide them. "Follow the route," the GPS said in a happy voice. Sean felt that this would be much easier, and this time, they would get there faster.

"We are lost," Jules told Greg.

"I hope not," Greg replied. Horror movies are made when families get lost on road trips. Have you seen those horror movies?"

Jules rolled her eyes. "Your imaginations are getting the best of you. It doesn't make you reasonable, one bit."

"Mom," Jules called.

"Look, kids, whatever squabble you have amongst yourselves isn't as important as our current situation," Dawn Brandice told her children.

"Are we lost?" Jules asked.

Their mom ignored the question as if she hadn't heard it or was thinking the same thing. She turned to her husband. Both of them had their eyes on the GPS. "Take the next left," the GPS demanded.

"I don't think that's quite right," Sean said. As he tried to turn right. "Recalculating. . . Recalculating. . . .," the GPS glared. Sean turned left. They were closer to the end of the road. Yet the left turn took them to a narrow path through the woods, with no other people or cars in sight. It all seemed strange until what they saw before them was a cliff, and there was nothing else in sight except the trees behind them.

"Mom, where are we?" Greg asked.

Even Dawn didn't have an answer to that. If anything, she was certain this wasn't the right place, yet the GPS kept blinking and saying, "You have arrived at your destination".

"This doesn't seem quite right. I'll be right back," Sean opened the door, leaving the kids in the car with their mom, and the headlights were on.

Dawn turned to the kids behind her. "It's going to be okay, guys. I think the GPS is broken."

"You have reached your destination," the GPS glared even louder than before.

"What in the hell is going on with this damn thing," Dawn blurted out loud.

"Mom, it has always been right, before. So why would it do this now," Greg said.

"Greg, I don't know, but one thing I know is that all of this will be over and we'll be able to go to sleep as soon as we get to the campsite. I know we're tired from the trip. Just hold on for a moment," she implored them, turning to see her husband a few yards away from the front of the car.

Suddenly, the car gave a weird jerky movement. Dawn was confused. She looked at her kids suspiciously.

"I didn't do that," Greg threw his hands up.

"Me neither," Jules clarified, also confused.

"Recalculating. . . . Recalculating. . .," the GPS glared. The car jerked again, the engine roared to life, and the wheels turned on their own.

"What the…"

Dawn ignored that her son was about to utter a cuss word. That wasn't a matter of urgency right now. What was shocking was the car working on its own; she grabbed the wheel immediately. The GPS tracker line increased by a few dots, indicating that their destination was in the front, yet there was nothing in front except the edge of a cliff.

"Recalculating. . .,"

She felt an unseen force push her from the wheel as the GPS blinked. Her body hit the passenger side door, and the children screamed in panic. They had no idea what was going on, and they couldn't hear their father despite his gestures.

The side windows rolled up on their own. It was as though they had lost control of the car.

"Recalculating. . . Recalculating. . ."

Dawn turned to Greg and Jules. "Everything is in control, okay? Kids…"

"Mom, the car is moving on its own. Make it stop! WHAT IS GOING ON?"

"I'm trying!" Dawn said while leaning over to push the brake pedal with her hand. Nothing was responding.

The car moved quickly, and without warning, the unexpected happened. The car raced at Sean and pushed him off the cliff. The GPS is still glaring, "Recalculating...."

Then everything went quiet. The children were too shocked to speak. Only Jules was hitting hard on the window, tears streaming down her face.

Dawn reached for her and held her against her chest, holding Greg with her other hand. The car creaked at the edge of the cliff, she closed her eyes.

"Recalculating... Recalculating..."

"Lord, help us," she said quietly.

The car jerked and pushed forward. "You have reached your final destination." The GPS said kindly. They fell to their deaths. Blood filled the windows of the car as their heads banged against the windows. It was a gory sight to behold.

CHAPTER 2

Tate had her headphones on and was looking at her phone as she walked into the kitchen where her mother was baking. She had been outdoors stretching since earlier and didn't know that Miles came to check on her. Her eyes were glued to her screen when she spoke.

"Mom, was Miles here earlier"? She looked up at her mother, Delilah Sherington, covered in flour and egg. It was hilarious, but she held back from laughing. It made sense when she saw Natalie, her twelve-year-old sister, holding the mixer with shock boldly written on her face. "What's happening?" Tate asked, pretending to be surprised.

"Your sister-"

"It was a mistake," Natalie said. "I'm sorry."

"Child! You're done with your baking lessons for today." Their mother tried to clean the flour from her face and body as she walked away from the table.

"What did you do?" Tate asked in a whisper.

Natalie looked down, sad. She dropped the mixer on the table. "I'm sorry, mom. I didn't know you told me to add water. It slipped my mind-"

"Natalie, you've got homework, don't you," mother asked. She had successfully cleaned off a bit of the flour and egg that was on her face. Tate still found this funny.

"Mom, this has to be the best natural clown makeup one would ever get."

She shot Tate a glare and hurled the towel in her hand at Tate's face.

"Urgh! Mom! Gross!" Tate shouted in disgust. Natalie said nothing to any of them. She left the kitchen. "Don't you think you were being too harsh on her?" Tate asked her mother.

"I didn't bring you up that way. You were a fast learner, and you made baking fun to teach," Mom said.

"We are different people. I might be skilled with baking, but Natalie does better with painting and other things. She beats me at it," laughed Tate.

Ms. Sherington sat by the table in the center of the kitchen where the flour and egg had splashed everywhere during her little baking class with Natalie. "I know, I know. I'm just worried she doesn't know what she wants to do yet, and her mind is all over the place. She is so flighty."

Tate smiled. "You worry too much, momma." She hugged her mother briefly. "She'll do better". Was Miles here, Tate asked?

"Oh! Yes, he was. It's just something I don't quite trust about him. He said you both were going hiking today, but you weren't picking up your calls. Child! What's going on with y'all?" Her mother asked, worried.

She understood why her mother was that way. She and Miles used to have little fights more frequently than any couple should. It bothered her mom and she always used to say, "Couples that are in love don't fight like that". But they were used to each other and Tate was committed to staying with Miles. She felt as if she loved him too much to let him go. Miles could be annoying, but he was also her best friend, and they had too much in common, from favorite meals to best colors, places of interest, and hobbies. He was her soulmate, and she was sure she could never find anyone like him.

"Yes, mom." Tate picked a cookie from the cookie jar. "He can be annoying sometimes, but we stick together, and we have our set routines…"

"Like holding a grudge and still hiking together, her mother said?"

Tate crunched a cookie and chuckled. "It's not a grudge."

"Well whatever you want to call it, child," her mother sounded displeased. "You say to-mato, I say ta-moto. If you're at least going to date, date right. Maybe y'all ought to consider counseling before going any further. Or-maybe find somebody else who is not an asshole."

"I'm not breaking up with Miles," Tate dropped the cookie and turned to leave.

"We are not done talking," her mother said.

"Miles will be waiting at the park. I'll see you later." She turned and pecked her mother on the cheek and ran out.

Tate wasn't ready to have that discussion with her mother. It was a sour topic. After all, it would ruin her mood for the day. Instead, Tate jogged down the street, smiling at everyone who cared to say hi to her. With the music playing loud in her ears, she let her mind wander from thoughts of her mother insisting she broke up with Miles, to what her friends thought of their relationship, to the strange incident that happened a few months back when Kayla and Dylan had gone missing after a night out.

There used to be six in their circle, Tate, Miles, Kayla, Dylan, Anton, and Debs. They thought they would be friends forever. Debs had left town since last Christmas to start on her acting career, and there were five of them left. Anton withdrew from the group when

Kayla and Dylan went missing, he was the closest to them. It wasn't easy for him to stick to the rest of them because somehow, their relationship reminded him of his friends who had gone missing. Tate wondered what life would have been like if they were all still together. She kept running, even at a faster pace now, until she had Miles in sight. His smile was as wide as anything; one would have concluded that their relationship was loving and smooth.

Tate slowed down as she arrived where Miles was waiting for her.

"You're late," he said casually, staring at his watch.

Tate ignored him. "How many minutes and how many laps today?" She asked, retying her shoelace.

"Fifteen minutes. Two laps...There's a mountain behind the park. Let's meet there when we are done," Miles said and pressed his hand over her shoulder, then he jogged off without saying anything else. That wasn't what Tate wanted. She wanted him to at least show concern and care about how she felt. Miles could be loving, but there were days when he just didn't care about how anyone felt, and these were days when she wished she had nothing going on with him. Her mother was right, but she was ready to try and prove her wrong.

She set off for the mountain. It would be their first time going there, but the adventure was worth it. She ran towards the forest behind the park, taking a route she had seen people take whenever they headed towards the mountain. She went through the wrong route and lost her way for a moment, her watch indicating that she was a few minutes behind the slated timeframe given to her by Miles. She was unfamiliar with the road, so she finally turned on the GPS. "Follow the highlighted route," it said. When she finally found her way to, she noticed that she was ten minutes late. Miles had always advised her to use the GPS whenever she suspected she was lost. But she hated blindly following the GPS. She thought it made people mentally lazy. For her, it was always better to develop your own sense of direction.

"Recalculating...." the GPS said kindly. Tate started moving in the direction of the "highlighted route".

As Tate started rushing because she didn't want to hear Miles' mouth about her being late, she tripped. "Shit," she whispered as she noticed that she scraped her knee. She wrapped it with a bandage that she always kept in her bag and kept running.

Miles was sitting on the ground close to the edge, with his eyes closed. He enjoyed meditating at every slight chance to experience silence.

"You're late," he said, his eyes still closed. "Getting lost isn't an option or a valid excuse. That's why you have the GPS."

"You know that doesn't show you care. You could have at least asked why I was late," Tate said. "Plus I'm using the GPS now"!

"Because it does change the fact that you're late. There's no better way to say it, Tate," Miles said sarcastically.

Tate was fuming at this point. She walked up to him, where he sat, and stood in front of him. She pulled off her headphone and dropped it on his leg. She started to leave until he pulled her back with his hand and stood to his feet.

"You're not breaking up with me, are you?" He asked.

Tate turned to him, so they were face-leveled. "You're annoying, Miles. I thought I could deal with it, but not anymore. Why don't you just leave me alone and go live your best life with someone who is always on your schedule. I'm done with this," she poked at his chest. She knew if her mother had been watching at that moment, she would have been proud of her.

"I love you, Tate."

"I don't care about that anymore," Tate told him point blankly. She ignored the trees dancing to the strange sudden wind that was blowing. "Go fuck yourself!"

Miles forcefully embraced her as she fought to break free from his hold.

"This wouldn't stop anything," Tate said, unimpressed. She hated that they were closer to the cliff's edge and all alone in a place she wasn't familiar with. "Miles, let me go."

"C'mon, you should know I didn't mean what I said. Fine, I overreacted, and I'm sorry," Miles apologized sincerely, but Tate wouldn't fall for his tricks. She lost count of the times that she had gone back on her words because of this emotional guilt trip that he often does and makes her change her mind. "Man! I'm trying my best, and you do not see the efforts. That's what pains me."

Tate stepped backward, chuckling. "You think I didn't know what you said about Kayla and Dylan back then. 'Dylan just wants to control her. She needs to break free from him. She's too good for him'. How are you any different? Miles, I really can't deal. I'm not in the best emotional state to deal with your drama." She attempted to leave, but Miles stood in her way, walking closer to her as she took some steps backward, closer to the cliff's edge.

"You have reached your destination," the GPS said.

Tate, now realizing that she forgot to turn it off and seeing how close she was to the edge, "Miles" she called out?

"Tate, please…" He raked his fingers through his hair, frustrated, and sighed.

"I've made up my mind."

He looked at her, hoping he would see the doubts dancing in her eyes, but her decision was so firm that he couldn't make her change her mind if he tried. "Fine," he moved out of her way to let her go.

Tate took a few steps forward, and that was when the ground rumbled beneath them. They both lost their balance, falling to the ground. They screamed. "Recalculating. . ." the GPS loudly announced. The ground shook again, and Tate screamed as her body rolled involuntarily off the cliff's edge. She almost fell off when Miles grabbed her hand while she dangled at the edge, screaming wildly with her eyes shut. She glanced at what was beneath her when her headphone fell off the cliff after Miles grabbed her. Beneath was dark, and she couldn't imagine what horror was waiting to welcome her if she had fallen. She suddenly hated the idea of hiking or the general idea of hanging out with Miles. Nothing had gone well in today's moments of them hanging out together.

She screamed again, wanting to look beneath her.

"Don't look," Miles said, grabbing her hand tightly. "Just look at me. Don't be scared...Okay?" he said to calm her down. The ground shook again.

"Why did you bring me here? To kill me?"

"The GPS suggested it was the best place to visit if I loved to hike.

Tate knew there was no lie about that; Miles was an explorer, and they both knew he had tendencies for such things.

Another big rock rolled past them and fell off.

Tate's GPS was still glaring loudly, "You have reached your destination!".

They waited for the sound of the rock, but it was so distant that they didn't hear anything. Tate could feel her heart beating in her throat. Was this how she would die? She had big dreams. Would she die without fulfilling any of these dreams?

"Recalculating," the GPS said.

"Miles!" Tate suddenly screamed as a big rock rolled from the top towards Miles' direction when he wasn't looking.

When he finally saw what Tate was calling his attention to, it was too late. The rock rolled at high speed, striking his head, crushing his skull and making his eyes pop out covering Tate's face with his blood.

She kept screaming and screaming with her eyes closed, gripping the sharper part of the cliff's edge tightly. She couldn't watch Miles' body fall off, so she kept screaming, hoping this was a nightmare that would end swiftly.

A coppery fluid slipped into her mouth; the taste of Miles's blood, she kept spitting it out, but that wasn't helping either. Her fingers hurt because the sharp edge of the rock was biting into her palm, causing it to bleed, and she didn't think she could hold on for much longer. She kept praying inwardly that someone would come to rescue her. If God could hear her prayers, she vowed to attend church more than she ever did because she didn't want to die.

Her hand slipped a bit, she began to cry, and her face had a mixture of tears and blood. She couldn't dare to stare beneath her. It would make her fear more for her life.

"You have reached your final destination," the GPS said in almost an evil laughing manner.

And the worst happened. The ground shook again, causing her to lose her grip on that sharp rock. All she knew the next moment was the wind was rushing against her face, and she was screaming wildly, falling to her death. As Tate is falling she wondered if anyone knew their death day or unconsciously walked into it. Because, if anything, she could have been more careful. Maybe tie up the loose ends in her relationship with people; her thoughts as she could feel the last part of her life leaving her. It was horribly unexpected, but it happened.

CHAPTER 3

Officer Ron with his last cigarette in his hand discarded it as he stepped out of the bar. He adjusted his glasses properly and walked to his car, parked afar off. He needed to drop by the station to see his superior, Captain Joe Jones, and the newbie they had brought in. He smiled to himself, remembering how he had gotten into the police force twenty years ago and how he'd be retiring soon. He couldn't wait to spend more time with his family, his granddaughter, most especially. He had invested so much in the force, putting in his best and never slacking for once. Although he had not been chanced at getting many promotions like any other privileged officers but, he at least offered good service to the neighborhood and put smiles on many faces, one way or the other.

His phone beeped. His wife was calling. A smile donned his face, as he tapped on the screen to answer.

"Chloe and her husband are coming this evening. Could you pick up some groceries on your way home from the station, his wife asked?"

Ron checked the weather; he knew it would rain but if he were to leave work early, then getting groceries would be possible. Rain or Shine, he still had to do it anyway because today was his thirtieth wedding anniversary, and his wife had done well to assume he didn't remember. That was the only occasion why Chloe and her husband would be traveling down, all the way from West Virginia to Georgia.

"Sure, honey. What else do you need?"

"Nothing else. Chloe will get us some bottles of wine," she said.

"What's the occasion?" He teased.

"Our anniversary," she replied. There was music playing in the background.

She always did that whenever she had work to do; it helped her concentrate.

"Oh yes! Our anniversary. How many years now?"

His wife paused. "Ron? You're growing old."

"No, I'm not," he said in self-defense. "Martha, I didn't forget, and you don't have to pull the old age card on me," he tutted. She had won this round.

Martha laughed out loud. It warmed his heart to hear her laughter. "Just come home early. The kids will be waiting."

"Alright," he answered and ended the call. Captain Joe's call came in right away.

"Been looking everywhere for you. Where are you?"

"At Marie's Bar. Heading to the station now," Ron told him.

"The newbie is here, waiting to fill in. I'll need you to brief him, and go through the file on your desk. I won't be here when you get back. I've got business to attend to downtown."

"Sure."

* * * * * *

Ron arrived at the station a few moments later. He thought he would be able to catch up with Joe, but he was met by the newbie.

"Joe's left?" he asked the newbie.

"Yes, sir."

He checked the files to see documents on missing identities and marked areas they were last seen. He trailed the marked regions with his index finger down to the center and paused, and then he looked up to see the newbie still standing at attention.

"Can you drive?"

"Sir, yes, sir!"

"Good. What's the name?"

"Sam. Sam Holly."

"Holly?" Ron sounded surprised.

"My mother named me after her mother when my father disappeared," Sam explained, still standing at attention.

"Oh! That explains it." Ron took a good look at him. Sam was a fine young man. It reminded Ron of when he was just a newbie like him in the police force. Back then, he was so naive and active. It took him making mistakes to realize that it wasn't about how much one could do but how well one could do the tasks assigned.

Welcome home, boy," he patted Sam on the shoulder. "You can leave. I've got this to go through," he said, referring to the document Joe left on his desk earlier.

"Yes, sir."

"You can take this with you," Ron said on a second note. He handed Sam some of his old files to become acquainted with those cases. "I'll put a call through if you are needed. Study the environment now, before work starts fully." Ron gave a smile. He had been doing this for years, making new officers comfortable in his company because he once wished he had an experience like that in his own time. Unfortunately, he never got such an opportunity and now seemed like the best time to let Sam enjoy his moment for a reason. He understood that Joe left the newbie behind to accompany him to the inspection site, but "I will do that on my own, leave the site and go home to meet my family", said Ron.

In no time, Sam left, and Ron glanced through the files. It had to do with everything concerning a missing family and two missing teenagers. For some reason, he found the teenagers familiar. He felt like he had seen them somewhere but couldn't remember where. Of course, it didn't help that he lost vital information like this. So he decided to get more details on the missing family instead.

The Brandice were a family of four; Sean and Dawn had been married for eleven years, with two kids, twins. They had a yearly ritual of camping out and spending time together so they could bond. But early this year, they went on the trip and never returned. It was strange enough that there was no trace of them anywhere.

Some witnesses claimed to have seen the family leave for the trip, but it was unusual for them not to return after two weeks. Ron now understood why the case was complicated, because one couldn't tell when the incident happened and how long it took them to find out. Yet, somehow, they assumed the case was linked to the two hikers that had gone missing a week ago and those teenagers.

Ron drafted something on a piece of paper. He intended to pay a visit to the home of the missing family, the teenager's parents, and the hiker's family. He thought of taking the newbie with him. But instead, he opened his drawer and picked up his gun. "Who knows?" Ron said, "one should always prepare for the worst".

He picked up the telephone on his desk and punched in some numbers. "Hi, Rosie…Can you have Sam report to my office immediately? Yes, Sam…The new detective."

He dropped the call, and Sam showed up at the entrance in less than five minutes. Joe hurled his car keys at him, "Familiar with the Brandice event?"

Sam caught the keys. He paused for a moment, then he nodded.

Ron smiled. "Great. We'll start there…"

They took Ron's car and drove, following directions to the Brandice's home. They lived in the countryside, close to the sea. And the serenity it gave confirmed how much they loved their space, with the need to explore.

"They loved quietness," Sam said.

Ron nodded in affirmation. They clambered out of his car and made it to the door in no time. They knew no one would answer if they knocked, but Ron still did. Sam stared at him, confused as if to say it was pointless.

"Pointless? I know. But courtesy demands that you knock before entering a stranger's home."

"But no one is there," Sam said.

"You never can tell, young man," Ron said.

He knocked the second time, and to their surprise, a response came from inside. They looked at each other in shock.

The door opened shortly to reveal a petite older woman with gray hair cut in a bobb. She was holding a cup of coffee and staring at them, unfazed. Ron tried to recall if there was anywhere in the Brandice's records that proved they had another relative in their home.

"Can we have a moment with you?" Ron asked.

The woman looked from Ron to Sam. She took a sip from her cup and nodded. Then she opened the door to let them in. When they entered, it looked orderly, almost like the family never left. There was something strange about being in the place, but Ron kept to himself. They followed her to the living room and stood.

"You may sit," she said.

"We won't be staying much longer. We just have a few questions for you."

"Go on, please," she dropped her cup on the table. There were pictures of the family hanging on the wall and art frames of abstract paintings. "I am Jane Brandice, Sean's great aunt."

Ron recalled that Sean's aunt was one of the meanest people in the whole town. When the family went missing, it seemed to ease her attitude a little.

"Ma'am what can you tell us about Sean and Dawn?"

"They were pretty happy, I guess. Even Though, I always thought that nobody could be that happy. Anyway, I never heard my nephew speak a cross word to her. They never had any serious issues. If they did, no one knew."

"Can you think of anyone who might be holding a grudge against them?"

"None." Aunt Jane thought for a while. "The trip was something they did yearly. Dawn always wanted me to stay here just in case one of those bad kids had to stay home. Normally when they act up, I make them come to my house and read. No TV and No technology. But this time my house is being remodeled, so I came here. I like it out here. It's really peaceful, except for the frogs making all that noise at night. I didn't feel right leaving to go home with them missing and all.

"You didn't take part in the investigation, did you?" Ron asked.

"No one knew I was here, but I kept calling their phones and none of them answered. It's been hard for me to accept because there is no explanation, no matter how reasonable it could be, that justifies them being missing. But, I know they are somewhere, and they will return soon," she said confidently.

Was there anything strange happening when they informed you of their trip?"

"The car, they weren't sure it would be fit for the trip. It kept giving them issues. Sean took it to have it looked at by the mechanic. It was, apparently, alright because that's the car they took. Now I do remember Sean talking about going to a new campsite. He pulled out the road atlas and other maps to find it. That's one thing I didn't like about that wife of his. She always depended on that technology. He was reading the maps and she just kept saying, 'we can GPS it'. I tell you that damn GPS is going to lead their ass astray one day".

"Yes Ma'am- ,"

"And another thing," Aunt Jane continued. "I think it was her idea to go to that new camp site. I don't see what was wrong with the old one. If I was going, I would've made them take me to the old one.

Sam noted this information down as Aunt Jane gave the illustration.

"Anything else out of the ordinary?"

"Nothing else that I recall," she answered with certainty. "I know they'll be back soon."

"Okay, ma'am. Thank you for your cooperation. We will reach out to you if there's anything else we need," Ron told her.

"I'll be here...I know they will return. Dawn will be back with her family; I'm waiting."

Sam shared a glance with Ron. It was as though they exchanged a message that they both understood. As soon as they stepped out, Sam spoke.

"She's delusional," he said.

Ron smiled briefly. It's in the records but not detailed. Everybody knows that Sean's Aunt Jane is crazy!

"Ohh!" Sam said with shock on his face. They returned to the car and drove to the Sharma's home, the next place they had to visit.

Sam scribbled some things he noticed about Jane Brandice in his notebook. It would be necessary for further investigation.

Arriving at the Sharma's, Kayla's father wasn't home. Kayla's mother was tending to her garden when the housekeeper informed her of their visit.

"Good day, Mrs. Sharma," Ron greeted with a smile.

"Hi, Ron. You never told me you would drop by today. But, unfortunately, Andrew isn't home," she told him.

"I came to see you...about Kayla and Dylan."

Kayla's mother frowned. "Oh! Why do we have to talk about that boy"? She gave a forced smile and said, "Can we have this talk over tea and biscuits instead?".

"I would love to but we don't have much time. You know today is my anniversary! I have a few more stops to make before I go home."

"Does Martha know about this? You know she hates it when you 'get lost' in your work."

"Sam, go on with the questions," Ron said distastefully. He was no longer interested in being there. It was because Mrs. Sharma was bringing up a past memory.

Sam was briefed on their way to the Sharma's home, so he knew what to do when Ron told him to go on with the questions.

"Mrs. Sharma, on the eleventh day of March, Kayla told you she was going for a walk, right?"

Mrs. Sharma shifted her gaze off Ron and nodded. "Correct, Officer."

"You mentioned earlier that you suspect a certain Dylan James, and coincidentally, he also went missing the same night Kayla disappeared. Is there anything you remember from that night that wasn't included in the statement you gave two months ago?"

"Has there been any new developments?" Mrs. Sharma asked with wide eyes expecting new information.

"We think the case might be related to Brandice's sudden disappearance and the two hikers that went missing three days ago," Ron broke the news to her.

Mrs. Sharma was confused. "So, what useful information do you have?"

Ron, standing up to leave, assured Mrs. Sharma, "We are working diligently on this case and we'll reach out to you if there's any other information we need."

Mrs. Sharma saw them at the entrance and watched them drive off in Ron's car.

"She doesn't seem to care that much," Sam said.

"Mrs. Sharma has always been like that. She has too much to worry about and the things that we think are important don't bother her." Ron glanced at his wristwatch, "You and I will visit Tate's mother tomorrow."

"Tate...The female hiker. Did the records say her mother has been avoiding every form of communication?"

"She's not in the right frame of mind. Tate is her favorite child, and she finds it hard to believe her child must have gone missing like the others," Ron told Sam.

Sam nodded and made a mental note to be cautious when it's time to see the woman. Finally, they arrived at the station, and Sam got out of the car, but Ron remained inside.

"I need to grab something for my wife. Tonight is our anniversary; she invited the kids, so she'll skin me if I don't make it home in time." He laughed.

Sam smiled. "Alright, sir."

* * * * * *

Ron hummed to the song playing on the radio. He smiled at the beautiful memories that replayed in his mind. The drive was lonely, yet he had never been that happy. Perhaps, because he would be seeing his grandchildren soon, he had always prayed to witness such a moment. He glanced at the trees by the roadside, and a familiar memory struck him. At night, he had seen two teenagers in a car on that lonely road. He couldn't get the girl's full name, but he could swear with his life that the girl was Kayla. His memory had never failed him. He was sure it was Kayla and Dylan that night. What could they have been doing on that road? And where did they go from there?

He pulled over at that spot where he had seen them and replayed the scene in his head. He told them to go home. But could they have gone home? What would he do if he were the guy? He realized he couldn't provide the correct answer, so he picked up his phone and dialed a number.

"Hey, Sam, buddy. Got a quick question for ya. Respond swiftly and with utmost sincerity. If you got caught in a car with your girl at night by an officer, and he told you to go home, what would you do?"

"Go to a secluded spot with her, where we won't be spotted easily," Sam responded.

Ron was staring at the woods by his side. He smiled to himself as soon as he got Sam's response.

"Bingo!" He got out of his car and walked into the woods, and to his surprise, he found faint car tracks in the dry mud. It must have been there for a while since the rain had not fallen in months. He followed the tracks, and they led him around a circle. *The kids got lost.* He took out his phone and turned on the GPS. It would help him cover the ground quicker.

"Follow the highlighted route," the GPS guided.

As he walked in the circle the GPS rerouted, "Recalculating."

This took him down a small trail, and it led him up a mountain where he found a phone. He looked around to see if there was anyone there.

"Hello?" No one responded. He picked up the phone and turned it on; but no response; it was dead. But a lettered sticker on the back read: T A T E. Ron couldn't believe his eyes. He suspected that the cases were related but had never been this close to being right. Perhaps, the perpetrator was playing mind tricks on him. He turned around swiftly when he heard a sound behind him.

"Who's there?" he asked again.

The GPS stated kindly, "You have reached your destination". He reached for his gun and pulled it out immediately. He heard a snap this time. "Show yourself!"

"You have reached your final destination"

As soon as he heard that, he couldn't believe what he saw next. A heavy rock fell from above and smashed his head. It rolled off the cliff with his lifeless body.

Martha would spend the rest of the night waiting for him. At first, she was very upset because Ron did silly things like this all the time. Showing up late just to make her worry about him. He always said it would make her appreciate him more. She called his phone over and over hoping he would answer, so she could cuss him out. She finally let her mind at ease and went to bed, knowing that he would come home in the middle of the night from either getting too caught up in his work or playing a silly joke. Martha knew that later she would be able to "give him a piece of her mind". She knew Ron was coming home. By morning, it would be too late to know that he was lying cold beneath a pile of stones like the others.

CHAPTER 4

Sam had woken up very late the following day. He rushed into the station and headed for Ron's office, hoping he would meet the old man there. But Ron's office was empty; Sam assumed he had gone to Ms. Sherington's home after waiting a long time.

"He's not in yet?" An officer asked from behind.

Sam turned and shook his head sideways. "He must have left for an interrogation," he told the officer.

"No. Ron has not been in the office since last night. That's strange. He never comes late to work," the officer said to himself and walked away.

Sam returned to his office, hoping he would drop by to check on Ron later. Instead, he got busy after an hour passed, he went to Ron's office, and ran into Captain Joe.

"Hey, seen Ron today?"

"Not yet," Sam answered, worried.

"Martha just called to check on him. She said he wasn't home last night for their anniversary party. She wanted to know why he wasn't answering his phone. She sounds like she has been crying."

"We returned together yesterday, and he said he was going to grab groceries on his way home for the party." Sam was confused as he spoke.

"That was all? You didn't hear them fight on the phone?" Joe looked more concerned.

"Not at all," Sam replied.

"Rosie!" Captain Joe called.

A lady rushed over. Sam had seen her around countless times. He assumed she was Joe's secretary. "Can you reach Ron and tell him to stop whatever prank he is up to? It's not funny anymore."

"Has he ever done this before?"

"Yea," Joe sounded distracted. His gaze was in Rosie's direction as if he was expecting her to return with feedback. "Some years back. He fought with Martha and went off the grid for two days. We were worried sick...Crazy man!"

"We can't reach him, Joe."

"Tell Andy to locate him with the chip. Be quick about it."

"What chip?" Sam felt lost, but he wanted to know what the chip was all about.

"Martha was worried the last time he went off the grid. So she asked me to track his phone," Joe explained.

"He could have changed the phone," Sam noted.

"He did. We deactivated it on the former and had it reinstalled in the present one." Joe smiled mischievously.

"Sir," An officer approached Joe, "one of our officers on patrol just reached out to us that they found a red car on the side of the road with no owner in sight. Someone in the neighborhood said it'd been there for hours. He-"

"What color?" Sam asked to confirm.

"Red," the officer answered. "The pictures just came in…" He looked in the direction of his computer. They followed him there to see the pictures on his screen.

"It's Ron's…" Joe trailed off. "Andy, zoom in that area."

Joe put Sam in charge of the case. Although he was a new detective, he always solved every case he was given. "Sam, just used Ron's office for now," Joe ordered. Then he dispatched the rest of the officers to help with the search.

* * * * * *

It's been days since they've been searching for Ron, and there has been no positive feedback yet. The search team lost their way through the woods and had to stop searching for a while. The tracker was not traceable.

* * * * * *

Sam stood by the door, watching Joe speak to Martha and Chloe. He could see the striking resemblance between Chloe's first child and Ron, and it was no wonder why he loved his grandchildren.

Joe walked toward Sam and patted him on the shoulder, signifying that it was time to leave.

"She is in a bad state. The news is also not helping," Joe said and shook his head. They stopped in front of his car. "What was the last thing Ron said to you?"

Sam tried to recall his memories from that day, and then he remembered vital information he had skipped. "After he left, he called me and asked: If you got caught in a car with your girl at night by an officer, and he told you to go home, what would you do?"

"Well, son, What did you say?"

"I told him we would hide where no one could find us," Sam answered. He blinked. "Could it be…"

"Sam, you are now in charge of this case. Take over from where Ron stopped. I have a hunch that his disappearance is linked to Tate Sherington, Kayla Sharma, and the Brandice family. Can I trust you with this? I know you're good at your job, but this is important...Can I trust you?"

"Yes, sir."

"I've heard good things about you, and Fred told me if ever I need someone to trust, you're the man for the job. Fred only speaks what's right; if he recommended you, then I can count on you. So help us find Ron... and solve this case. Let me know if there's anything you need," Joe said. He got in his car and drove off.

Sam stood for a moment. He looked back at the house and wondered how many memories Ron had locked in the house. He seemed happy. He was a happy man. Sam had heard nothing but good about him, and it was enviable and disheartening that he never got to spend more than a short moment with the man.

Some officers came out of the house, Ben and Frank. They were talking to each other until they looked up and saw Sam.

"Hey, Sam. Chloe wants to see the officer in charge of the case," Ben said.

"Alright." He left them and walked towards the house. That wasn't until he heard Frank say something quietly.

"He's the new detective from Harolds. Joe trusts him. Joe says that an old friend referred him...Well, let's see how long he lasts." Then Frank chuckled.

Sam wondered what that could mean. But he had been in the field for a while. He couldn't be bothered by it.

Chloe observed Sam at the entrance and took fast strides towards him, pulling him into a spot where her mother couldn't see them.

"Tell me everything you know. I want nothing but the truth. Trust me, I can handle it," she glanced behind her, "What I can't do is sit and watch, not knowing what exactly happened to my father."

Joe had briefed Sam about Chloe. She was nosy and tough like her father and would never take no for an answer.

Sam comforted, "Chloe, the police are trying hard to locate Officer Ron. We have nothing concrete yet, but I will inform you if there's anything. Speak freely with everyone. We might be able to get something from there."

Chloe looked disappointed, as though the moment she approached Sam, he would have the answers to her questions.

Sam took that moment to ask one last question of Chloe. He knew how close Ron and Martha were, and it was only fitting that he asked this question to clear all doubts.

"One more thing," Sam said. Chloe looked at him attentively, "How close were your parents? Did your father talk about work with your mother?"

Chloe replied swiftly. "It was an unspoken agreement never to discuss work at home."

Sam, trying to write something. Assured Chloe that he will do everything he can to solve this case. "In the meantime, stay around and take care of your mother. Keep her company. She'll need it now more than ever."

Chloe gave him a faint smile, and Sam left. Sam knew what she wanted was the raw truth, but he didn't have any of that to offer her. So instead, he hoped they would soon get to the bottom of the case.

CHAPTER 5

Ms. Sherington, in tears, sniffed for what seemed like the umpteenth time since the arrival of Detective Sam. She bawled her eyes out. Natalie, comforting her, handed her the last box of tissues as she looked up at Sam.

Sam watched and waited for her to speak. He wouldn't want to be represented as the inconsiderate detective who wouldn't let the grieving mother mourn.

"I'm so sorry you had to see me this way." She sniffed. "What can I offer you?" She asked and glanced at Natalie.

Sam raised his hand as if to stop her. "Oh no! I'm okay. I won't be staying for long. I just need you to answer a few questions, and I'll get going."

Ms. Sherington sat up straight. Looking weak and distraught compared to a framed picture of her on the wall. "Experiencing the loss of a love one can have a damning effect on one's physical features," said Natalie.

"Ma'am, can you narrate what happened the last time you saw Tate?"

She looked at Natalie; Natalie nodded and turned back to the detective. She stared at her fingers as she spoke. "She went on a hike. She always did that with that boy…" Her voice changed.

"Which boy?" Sam asked, curious.

"Miles Cornata," her voice softened. "It's just something about him that I didn't trust!"

"Did you two happen to fight before she left on the hike?"

"No…"

"Mom," Natalie called.

"It wasn't a fight. I didn't exactly approve of her going with that boy on a hiking trip while they were mad at each other. But as always, Tate was willing to do anything to prove me wrong. She was adamant. She left before I could 'steal her joy'".

Was that all?" Sam eyed her.

"Yes," Natalie answered. "I was here."

"Good…Natalie, what do you know about Miles and Tate's relationship?"

"She"…Natalie waited in thought.

"They were cool," she spouted.

Sam looked at her, waiting for more. "Continue, Natalie. I'm not going to tell anyone what you say here."

"I don't know," she shook her head. "Tate didn't want me to tell mom. But she says sometimes, Miles doesn't treat her right. Yes, they were best friends and all that, but he did things and said things that sometimes hurt her."

"Physically?" Sam asked, taking notes.

"I don't think so."

Tate's mother looked shocked. She had no idea what was going on between Miles and Tate. "How come no one told me this?"

"Tate said to keep it secret," Natalie replied.

"But she's dead now. The boy killed her and hid her body. He killed her!" Her voice raised.

"Ma'am, we can't be so sure anyone is dead. But, as you can see, we are doing our best to find these kids."

"I know about the missing family and Kayla Sharma. They were never found. What gives you the assurance you'll find my daughter? You know the truth. The truth is that they are gone forever."

"Mom!" Natalie shouted at her. "Stop this, okay! Please! Anton has been feeding you with lies." Natalie faced Sam. "You have to leave now. Please…"

Sam stood and bowed. "Thank you, ma'am. Natalie, thank you." Natalie walked him to the door. As soon as he stepped outside, he spotted a hooded guy on the other side of the picket fence. Sam pretended not to see him, as he turned back to Natalie.

"If anyone drops by or if you hear anything, let me know," Sam said.

Natalie nodded.

Sam looked in the direction of the hooded guy and realized he had disappeared. Someone was either stalking him or Tate's family. He returned to the station, linking all the information he had gotten from the victims' families.

Ben peeking into Sam's make-shift office, which is Ron's. "Hey, man!" "How's it going?"

"Stuck." Sam mumbled. He was distracted, connecting dots, but something was missing, and he just couldn't figure out what it was.

"Wish I could help," Ben said.

Sam didn't know how sincere that was, but he could use all the help he could get, which could only be from someone familiar with these victims and their families.

"Come in," Sam said.

Ben didn't understand what Sam said. He still stayed by the door.

"Ben," Sam looked at him and gestured for him to come in.

Ben entered, looking around as though he was in a strange environment. He saw the crime wall on which Sam pinned pictures of victims from the missing case. There was the Brandice family, Kayla Sharma and Dylan James, Tate Sherington and Miles Cornata, and Officer Ron Jessie beneath their names.

"If my little cousin were here, I would have feared for her life," Ben said.

Sam looked up from the documents on his desk. "Why did you say that?"

"I mean, can't you see the connection?"

"What connection?"

"Kayla, the delivery boy, Dylan, Tate, and Miles used to be close friends. They had a group before my cousin left town," Ben said.

"What's your cousin's name?"

"Deborah. Debs. She called me last night asking about them all, but I couldn't tell her about Miles and Tate because that would be bait to get her back here. Who knows what is happening around here? I cannot afford to risk that."

"Don't you find it strange that she's suddenly asking about them?" Sam was driving somewhere. He was more interested in the discussion than ever. He wanted to meet someone who could give him information about these victims.

Ben's face contorted into a frown, and Sam took that opportunity to probe more.

"Someone has been feeding her with the details, but enough to get her curious, if you ask me," Sam said. He hoped what he did worked.

"I'll kill that rat, bastard," Ben muttered. "I knew he was up to no good since I started seeing him around lately."

"Who's that?"

"Anton."

The name rang a bell in Sam's memory, and he didn't know where he had heard it. "Who's Anton?"

"He was the last friend who didn't fit in their circle. The socially awkward one. Gave off a strange aura. I don't know why Debs always defended him."

Stop this, okay? Please. Anton has been feeding you with lies.

"Anton!" Sam shouted. "Ben, I need more information on Anton."

"The boy was a loner, despite being friends with the kids. He suddenly disappeared when Debs left."

"How did you know?" Sam asked.

"Are you interrogating me?" Ben sounded offended.

"No, Ben. I think we have our guy, and if we do, you contributed greatly to this case. So help me out here," Sam pleaded.

Ben looked around and spoke in whispers. "My little cousin wanted me to keep an eye on him, but he suddenly disappeared and never showed up until days after Kayla's incident. I didn't see him again after that, so I assumed I was mistaken. Recently, I must have sighted him in the park with his red hoodie. Strange kid," Ben muttered.

"Red hoodie. Does this hoodie have stripes of black on the arms of it"?

"Yes! Yes! Debs got him that hoodie for Christmas. He has been wearing it since then," Ben said.

Sam picked up his phone and called Natalie's line. He wasn't listening to Ben anymore. "Natalie. It's Sam. Listen to me, and respond just with a Yes or No. Do you understand"?

"Yes," Natalie responded.

"You knew about Anton?"

"Yes."

"Did he ever ask Tate out?"

"Yes."

"Was that after she started dating Miles?"

"No."

"While they were all cool, did he come to your place more often than the rest?"

"Yes."

"Did your mother sincerely like him?"

"She found him pathetic but cared for him still."

"Natalie!"

"I'm sorry. I wanted to explain…" She paused.

"Natalie, who's that?" her mother asked on the other side.

"A friend, mom."

"Alright. Anton is here to see you."

"Natalie," Sam called. "Be yourself. Be natural. Delay him for as long as you can, but be careful." The call dropped.

"Anton is our guy?" Ben asked.

"One more thing I need to confirm." Sam left the office, and Ben followed him. "Andy!" He called a guy when he got to the central intelligence unit.

Andy approached him. "Hey, Sam. Is there something you need me to help you with?"

"Quick question. At the crime scene in the woods, we went in circles for hours and couldn't go beyond the tracked region, yet we couldn't find Ron. What are your presumptions?"

"I told Joe earlier that someone was messing with the location tracker. We've got our system hacked three times now; and do you know what's more interesting about this. These were the three times our victims went missing. But I wasn't certain, so Joe discarded it. Until a few minutes ago, when it got hacked again and I could track the location before it disappeared. I was coming to see you."

Sam looked at Ben, confused and shocked. "Where's the location?"

"You won't believe it. Tate's home."

Sam's eyes widened with shock. "Dispatch every patrol officer within that region to Tate's home. We have our guy."

"Our guy? Not the girl?" Andy was confused.

"Anton," Ben said.

"Holy Christ!"

"Is he trying to get back at the police force for rejecting him last year?" Finn, Andy's colleague, asked.

Sam looked from Ben to Andy. "What's that?"

"He took the exams and passed with flying colors. But when he took the psychological exam, the doctor said that something wasn't quite right. So he wasn't able to get it. Captain Joe could've let him in but he decided against it. Anton was pissed off. He came in throwing tantrums talking about how we all would pay for rejecting him. Ron was able to calm him down. He always had a way of calming people down. Anton was quite a handful," Finn replied. "But he was good with technology. Really good. His ass probably hacked into our tracking system. That's why everything has been off lately. That crazy mother- ".

"Oh...It makes sense now." Sam was more certain. He got his team ready, and they headed to Tate's house.

They found a bike outside the house against the picket fence. After ensuring the house was surrounded by officers, Sam signaled the backup team to take caution while he went in with Ben.

Sam could hear sobs as he quietly and slowly made footsteps down the hallway to the living room. As he drew closer, he realized it was the sound of someone whimpering. He came into full view of the room and saw Ms. Sherington tied to a chair, struggling to break free. Her mouth was taped, and her hands were tied. She kept fighting and with widened eyes, she was trying to say something. They couldn't understand her because her mouth was gagged. The first thing Sam did was remove the tape from her mouth while Ben looked around.

"He's...gone," she managed to say.

Ben returned to the living room. "There are no signs of Natalie. But his bike?" Ben was confused.

Tate's mother took a slow breath before letting her words out. "He...took her away in my car."

Sam realized he didn't see the car when they drove in. "Your car?"

"It's always parked in the garage. Tate and the kids..." She coughed. Ben offered her water, "Thank you," she took a sip and continued talking. "They used to mess around in the garage. Anton once fixed the car, so he knows his way around."

"He got away with the car. He bought himself time, leaving his bike outside," Ben glanced at his watch.

"Ma'am, is there anything else you want us to know?" Sam asked. His men trooped in.

"He uses Caltoosio Magic," Tate's mother seemed shocked, more like she didn't believe what she had said.

"At first, I thought it was just something stupid Anton made up like he always does. But after talking to my friend Professor Butler, I realized that it's one of the most powerful evil forms of witchcraft anyone could practice. And No! Anton probably didn't learn it all because he's always half-assing".

"I may need to have a word with this Professor," Sam noted.

Sam looked at his guys and instructed them to watch over Tate's mother. Then he left for the backyard. The garage was open with evident tracks of a car driven out. Sam wondered how long Anton had planned this all out. There was a connection between the victims, Anton's Caltoosio Magic, and that wooded area. Sam just couldn't quite figure it out yet.

"Let's follow the tracks," he called out to two of his men with Ben. They trailed the tracks down a path leading to the woods behind the Sherington home; it became clearer as they trod the path. Linking them to the path where they found old car tracks from Kayla's incident. Anton's hideout was in the woods, and he managed to get away with everything he did because no one suspected him.

"Stay here," Sam instructed Ben and another officer while he scouted with someone else. They had gone around for minutes and still returned to the same spot. Sam turned on his phone and tried using the GPS to locate the nearest building or possible hiding spot. There was no signal so his GPS app kept loading and never coming on. He knew if he could find a network, then he could find Anton's hideout which was close by. Finally, he turned to Ben and tapped his shoulder. "The path is unclear because he is trying to hide his tracks. This has to be it". He showed Ben a path. They could never have suspected it to be Anton's route. The two of them went down the path and saw a cave afar off.

"We found him," Ben said.

"We can't be too sure," Sam replied, then he pulled out his gun and cocked it.

CHAPTER 6

There was smoke rising out of the cave, Sam and his men were unbothered. Sam had witnessed worst scenarios, but never expected to hear groans and chants with a pitched humming sound. He remembers what Ms. Sherington said about Anton practicing the Caltoosio Magic.

He paused at the entrance, pointing his gun before him. He heard Ben talk to someone over the phone.

"The Beta team discovered a mountain top, and the GPS led them there. They will be there to search the entire place," Ben explained.

Sam nodded in response. If he were to hear movement, he would shoot whomever or whatever was down there.

"Stay back," he signaled to his men. He stepped further into the cave and felt his phone chime in his pocket. He raised it to see his GPS app flashing. Whatever Anton was doing inside had an effect on his GPS. But how could this be? Is Anton's magic controlling the GPS?

When Sam got deep into the cave and saw the lit candles forming a circle, and Natalie in a spot, tied up, he feared for his life. Not because Anton could harm him, but because of the hideous figurines hanging on the wall with Anton in the middle of them, deeply engrossed in his chants. Anton danced around in a circle, swaying his arms, and jumping up and down on his toes. Sam could have never believed that this boy was so diabolical. Then, right before his eyes, a cloud of smoke came out of the ground, taking the form of an unknown being.

"Go, go," Anton said, and Sam watched the smoke escape.

Reflexively, Sam ran outside of the cave. Seeing the direction of the smoke, he fished out his phone to see his GPS fluctuating.

"What's going on?" Ben asked.

"Get Natalie out of there. Hold down the boy. This case is more serious than we thought it was," he explained to Ben. Right then, they heard a heavy thud, as they took a step forward, their phones rang simultaneously. Ben glanced at Sam answering the call first. Not saying a word, Ben had shock written all over his face.

"We just lost one of our men," Ben announced.

"How?" Sam was curious. He was sure Anton was still in the cave.

"You won't believe it," said Ben. Looking confused, "They said a wisp of smoke moved a big rock, and the rock rolled over him."

"What?! We are taking that boy with us. Go get the girl out," Sam instructed some of his men that had just arrived.

Same made his way to the cliff and couldn't believe what he was seeing with his own eyes. Whatever Anton was doing in the cave affected everyone's GPS. Whenever someone's GPS is close to the cliff's edge, it kills them. It suddenly hit Sam, that the other victims had unknowingly fallen prey to this.

※ ※ ※ ※ ※ ※

Sam returned to the station exhausted and slightly pissed. He asked for Anton.

"Where is that rat bastard?" he asked Ben. "Let me calm down," Sam said doing some deep breaths.

"In the interrogation room, but that boy won't say a word" said one of the officers.

"We will make him talk whether he likes it or not," Sam said, as he headed to the interrogation room.

Because of his desperation to find the truth, the interrogation room was a place where Sam often lost every form of himself. Any suspect who encountered Sam in this form always feared him, and it usually didn't take long before he could break them. Sam walked into the interrogation room with two cups of coffee. He dragged the seat opposite of Anton and sat in it, placing the coffee on the table between them.

"Hello, Anton. I got you coffee," Sam announced as if Anton couldn't see the obvious.

Anton didn't budge. He didn't acknowledge Sam's presence. Instead, his gaze was on the CCTV camera fixed at the corner of the room.

"Hey, Anton. I'm a friend, and with that being said, I came to hold a friendly conversation with you." Sam took a notepad and placed it on the table with his pen. "I need you to answer a few questions and that would be all for now."

Anton still didn't budge; he seemed determined to stay mute for as long as possible.

Sam moved closer, "I know you did it...all of it, and I'm going to find out how."

Anton began to chuckle but Sam was unfazed; he had seen crazier criminals and he broke them all.

"Who was Tate to you?" Sam asked.

Anton was quiet. Then he looked Sam in the eye, "Fuck you! I'll kill you too."

"Anton, let's start over. You're not being accused of anything. I just need to get my facts right, and I need you to help me here. Is that clear?"

"Who was Tate to you, Anton Marreck?"

"Don't call me that!" Anton's tone was harsh and pitched.

Sam raised his hands. "Good, good. No names. Who was Tate?"

Anton tapped on the table with his fingers, and then he began to talk. "She was mine before they all came."

"Who were the 'they'?"

"The stupid family. Kayla, Dylan, and Miles…"

"And the police?"

"It wasn't planned," Anton said.

"What wasn't planned?" Sam pretended he didn't need the information, but he was recording every word.

"I don't know. I don't have control over what the spirit does. It's an ancestral spirit of revenge brought on by the Magic."

"That was real? Was the Caltoosio Magic you practiced in the cave real?" Sam asked.

Anton laughed. "What did you think it was? Theatrics. My friends didn't like me because they discovered this part of me, but I couldn't let it go knowing they wouldn't sacrifice that much for me. So what's the point?"

"If you liked Tate that much, why then did you kill her?" Sam asked.

"I didn't want to kill her. She wasn't meant to be there. She told me she wouldn't go hiking that morning. I thought her mother could persuade her, but she didn't listen and-"

"What did the family do so wrong?" Sam inquired. Thankful that he was getting some answers out of Anton without using force.

"They said Tate and Miles were a perfect match. How could they?"

Sam looked at him for a moment and stretched his lips into a smile; it was becoming vivid.

"You eliminated your man..."

"I don't kill," Anton corrected.

"Your spirit," Sam replied. "How does it work?"

"I invoke the spirit to manipulate the nearest GPS, taking them to the cliff where they meet their fate. I killed no one...The spirit avenged me."

Sam hit his fist on the table. "Does it look like I'm joking with you?" Anton was taken aback. "You did all this, but you still claim to be innocent."

Anton had withdrawn to his usual self. When he began to open up, he would not look Sam in the eye.

Sam saw the misery and sadness etched on Anton's face; he almost fell for his deception.

"Why Natalie?" Sam asked.

"She talks too much."

"You're a psycho," Sam said, but Anton laughed maniacally. Sam dragged him close, pressing his chest against the table. "How do you stop this? You killed one of my men and all those other people. Officer Ron, the only one who was in your corner. I don't understand why you find this funny."

"Because I can't help you," Anton said amidst his grunt. "There's nothing I can do to stop it."

"Huh?" Sam was confused. "Why not?"

Anton began to laugh. "The spirit follows my orders, but I can't make the magic undo itself. I can't help you, Detective Sam."

Sam, in shock, reached for Anton's neck. "You're a dumb ass. Why the hell would you do magic and not know how to undo it? You're just like Ms. Sherington said, "You're always half-assing stuff. You never take the time to do anything right."

"She did not say that! She loves me," Anton answered.

"Yeah she did! You can't even do magic right! Dumb Ass!"

"I'll show you! Wait until I get out of here and I'll show how much of a dumb ass I am and I'll show that bitch too!" Anton screamed.

"You won't be getting out of here anytime soon!" Sam exclaimed.

Detective Sam stopped the interrogation and left the room. Joe was the first to meet him outside.

"Were you able to get anything out of him?"

"He's responsible for all their deaths but doesn't agree to be directly involved. He says a spirit he invoked while doing Caltoosio Magic took control of everybody's GPS that went to the woods and caused all of their deaths. This is so messed up." Sam said while shaking his head.

"Could it happen again?" Joe looked worried with a frown on his face and his brows arched.

"That's the bad news. Yes, he can't stop it. There's a possibility we might lose someone else to this foolishness again very soon. I don't trust this kid."

"Who then do you trust?" Joe asked randomly, and something clicked in Sam's memory.

"Good question. I know someone who can help us out," he said.

"Go on, then." Joe was relieved.

Sam went to his office and sat in front of his PC. He knew the website. He remembered the Professor in Witchcraft and Demonology, which Ms. Sherington told him about. Normally Sam would think stuff like this is just foolishness. But now after seeing it with his own eyes, he is a believer. He went straight to Banto A & M University, to the office of Professor Butler.

* * * * * *

"Hello Detective Holly," the Professor greeted with his tortoise shell glasses over his eyes. He seemed to know that Sam was coming.

"Hi, Professor. I need your help, and I'll go straight to the point," Sam said, as the Professor nodded. Sam began to tell the story of the missing people who have died and narrated his interrogation with Anton.

The Professor sighed and explained. Caltoosio Magic is the most deadliest form of magic there is. It has always been my fear that someone who didn't know how to control it would learn about it and try to use it. The Caltoosio people were brought here as slaves. They were treated so badly by the slave masters that one day they called on this spirit of revenge. It took over all the plantations in the area. There were unexplained reports of slave masters and their families going missing. So the town's people rounded up all the slaves and burned them alive because they blamed the slaves for the strange happenings and missing people. However, they didn't realize that they released the spirit of revenge to be invoked at any time by anyone who knows how to. If someone is well versed in invoking the spirit, they can call it back once they feel avenged. If the person that invoked the spirit doesn't know how to call it back;

the only way to stop this chaos is by a bullet in the head of the one who invoked the spirit. That's why I'm so fearful, said Professor Butler. That is the only way to stop more chaos.

"Thank you, Professor Butler. I really hope Anton can call this spirit back," sighed Sam as he headed back to the station.

Sam returned to the interrogation room, intending to have Anton call back the spell. He didn't want anyone else to die because of this stupid spell.

"Anton, I know I got a little angry with you before and I'm sorry. I really need you to call back the spell."

"Oh! Who's the dumb ass now? You need me. I knew you would come running back to me for help."

"Okay," Sam said sheepishly. "I'll be the dumb ass for today, just say you can call it back".

"Sure I will."

"Okay, you're coming with me," Sam said as he ordered some of his men to bring Anton to the woods. None of them used their GPS as they were scared that the Caltoosio spirit of revenge would attack. So they each got there at separate times. They took Anton out of the car and took him to the cliff where the spirit often killed its victims.

"What do you want from me?" Anton kept fighting back.

Sam raised his gun at Anton to scare him, with others watching. "You'll do what I ask you to do. Or I'll kill you where you stand."

Anton didn't know that the only way to call back the magic was by putting a bullet in the head of the person doing the magic; so he kept being sarcastic. He didn't really believe Sam would shoot him.

"Do it," Sam advised. "Call it back now".

"You're joking, right?" Anton glanced at their faces. "I can't break it. I don't know how to."

"But you placed it, so break it. Go on," Sam said.

Reluctantly, Anton stepped forward and began to chant. His chants became louder, and the wind blew ferociously, howling in their ears. The officers were falling over and blowing away. Something was strange. It was as though Anton was doing another thing entirely. Anton was doing the same dances and chants as before but this time louder and more fierce. The smoke started to rise. The wind started to blow as if it were a hurricane or tornado. Sam eventually realized he was calling the spirit to kill everyone there. When Sam saw the smoke racing towards him; he sadly lifted his gun and shot Anton right in the center of his forehead. The smoke and wind subsided as Anton fell to the ground and everywhere became calm.

Everyone understood what just happened. The ambulance arrived shortly, and Sam scouted the area with his men before leaving for the station. The coroner was carrying Anton out on a stretcher covered by a white sheet. As Sam and Ben walked by, Anton's body sat up by reflex and he said, "I WILL BE AVENGED". He then flopped back down on the stretcher dead.

It seemed like the end, but it wasn't.

Detective Holly knew better!

9 7 9 8 9 8 6 4 5 0 1 2 4